Dream With Diosa

N.C. Royale

AuthorHouse™
1663 Liberty Drive
Bloomington, IN 47403
www.authorhouse.com
Phone: 833-262-8899

Because of the dynamic nature of the Internet, any web addresses or links contained in this book may have changed
since publication and may no longer be valid. The views expressed in this work are solely those of the author and do
not necessarily reflect the views of the publisher, and the publisher hereby disclaims any responsibility for them.

Any people depicted in stock imagery provided by Getty Images are models,
and such images are being used for illustrative purposes only.
Certain stock imagery © Getty Images.

This book is printed on acid-free paper.

ISBN: 978-1-6655-6891-3 (sc)
ISBN: 978-1-6655-6892-0 (hc)
ISBN: 978-1-6655-6890-6 (e)

Library of Congress Control Number: 2022915590

Print information available on the last page.

Published by AuthorHouse 08/26/2022

authorHOUSE®

This Book is dedicated to my dazzling daughter Diosa, you are my dream come true.

Wink Wink
Blink Blink
Diosa is off to sleep.

Can you see what type of dream
Diosa is about to dream?

In this dream there will be gold
stars that shine so bright,
Pink and blue clouds that bounce in the sky,

Sparkly unicorns
racing through
the air,

5

Dancing fluffy llamas
with crystals in their hair,

6

Buzzing bumble bees
floating through
palm trees,

And orange and green children eating pink ice cream.

She'll ride neon rainbows up the mountain top,

9

Jump on lily pads and make baby frogs hop.

10

She'll dive into
waterfalls filled with
purple whales,

Skip on magic
beaches covered with
singing seashells.

12

In this dream, everything
Diosa imagined is what
Diosa could see.

She could grab it
with her hands or
feel it under her feet.

14

Then over her head floated
a huge peach balloon,
It was so big that it carried
her to the moon.

16

The moon was the brightest
thing that she had ever seen,
There were shooting stars, rocket
ships and planets with rings.

Although she was happy to see
everything from above,
It was still just a dream, no
family there to love.

20

With a wink wink
and a blink blink
Diosa woke up
from her sleep.

Can you remember all of the things
Diosa saw in her dream?

About the Author

N.C. Royale dreamt of many things as a child born in Long Beach, Ca. Many of her dreams did come true, such as modeling, singing, acting and writing. She wrote her first novel " Roses With Thorns" at the tender age of 15. She later studied film at Clark Atlanta University. That is when she began her dream of writing screenplays for film festivals. It took her biggest dream of all, her dazzling daughter Diosa, to inspire her to write "Dream With Diosa", her first children's book. Royale currently lives amongst the peaches of Atlanta, Ga with her family, Where she continues to dream. She can be reached at ncroyalebooks@gmail.com.

Printed in the United States
by Baker & Taylor Publisher Services